SUPERHERO SON

WRITTEN BY

CHARIS SELFRIDGE-POOR

In a seemingly quiet house, on a seemingly quiet street,
Lives a superhero son whose world seems incomplete.

1

He has all these abilities to run and leap and soar,
But for now, his mother tells him that he must use
them indoors.

2

"But Mum, a superhero's work cannot be done inside!
I can't rescue planes or speeding trains if I stay here and hide.

You know, I'd use these powers to help, if only I were able!"
He bellows at his mother while she lays the kitchen table.

"Just watch me swing across the room!" he says then demonstrates,
Diving off the kitchen counter and clattering all the plates.

His mother swooshes past and catches them before
they fall,
Then fires a withering look at him that simply says it all.

"Well, I also have this super speed!" in a blink he disappears,
Running to collect the toys and stack them up in tiers.

7

His mother smiles and thanks him with a look of pure delight.
As the toaster smokes then – POPS! Giving her a little fright.

"Let me help!" he says, shooting sticky strands at the ceiling.
The toast clings there with white stringy hair, now looking unappealing.

"Wait! I also have super strength." He grabs for the tight-lidded jar,
Karate chopping off the lid, spraying green gunk near and far.

"What about this?" In a whirlwind he spins, sending everything flying. Then, he laser beams the twins' cold food. With burnt tongues, they both start crying.

12

In a blur his mum darts from here to there,
Catching the toast that's dangling mid-air.

13

She dries the twins' tears and cools down their food
While restoring the room and her much calmer mood.

Her son slumps in his chair, feeling somewhat morose.
"My powers are meant for more than just rescuing toast!

It doesn't seem fair, being stuck here at home,
Not helping those people out there on their own."

Then his mum hears him say from his muffled rant,
"I just wanted to make you proud, but I can't."

17

On a discarded grape, she turns and slips,
As the baby's highchair starts to tip!
Superhero son, springs into action,
Lunging with his speedy reaction!

In a flash, he's at his mother's side,
Catching her waist and up-righting her stride.
His legs strike out and push back the chair,

Then catapult him into the air.

Summersaulting twice, he aces the landing,
Surveying the room with a fresh understanding.

23

With his brothers safe and his mother shaken,
He's so glad he was there to help this situation.

His mother then says, with her arms out wide,
A look of relief and so much pride,

"You know, you may not always save the day,
But helping out in other ways

Is what makes a superhero, you see,
And my son, you mean the world to me."

"So it's true, you have abilities to soar, leap and run,
But sometimes at home you're needed most,

You, our Superhero Son!"

Printed in Great Britain
by Amazon